G.I. JOE
AT
PEARL HARBOR

G.I. JOE AT PEARL HARBOR

James Kelley

SCHOLASTIC INC.
New York   Toronto   London   Auckland   Sydney
Mexico City   New Delhi   Hong Kong   Buenos Aires

ISBN 0-439-35574-5

12 11 10 9 8 7 6 5 4 3 2 1   1 2 3 4 5 6/0

Printed in the U.S.A.

First Scholastic printing, September 2001

Contents

G.I. JOE AT PEARL HARBOR

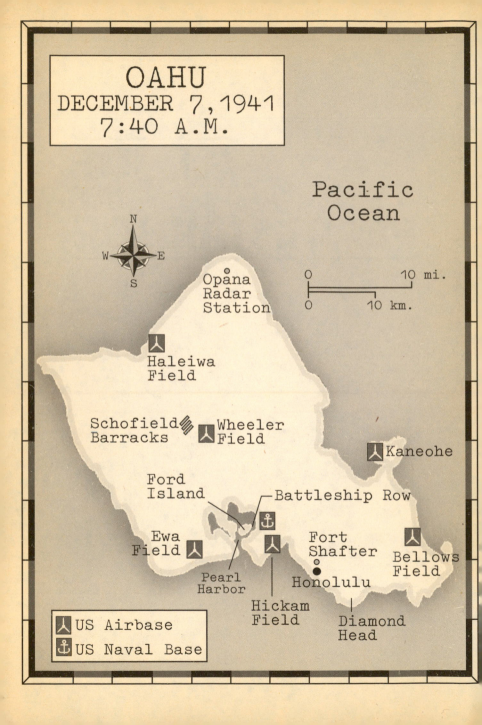

PEARL HARBOR
DECEMBER 7, 1941
7:40 A.M.

0   1/2   1 mi.

Pearl City

DETROIT

Ford Island Naval Air Station

RALEIGH

UTAH

Aiea Bay

BATTLESHIP ROW

ARIZONA   ← NEVADA

← VESTAL

TENNESSEE   ← WEST VIRGINIA

OKLAHOMA

← MARYLAND

CALIFORNIA

Oil Storage

FORD ISLAND

Pearl Harbor

N
W   E
S

SHAW →

DESTROYER DOCKS

SUBMARINE PENS

Hospital Point

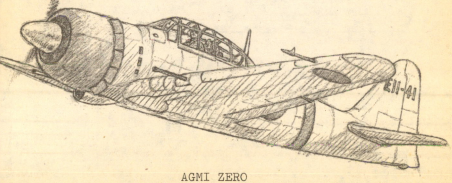

AGMI ZERO

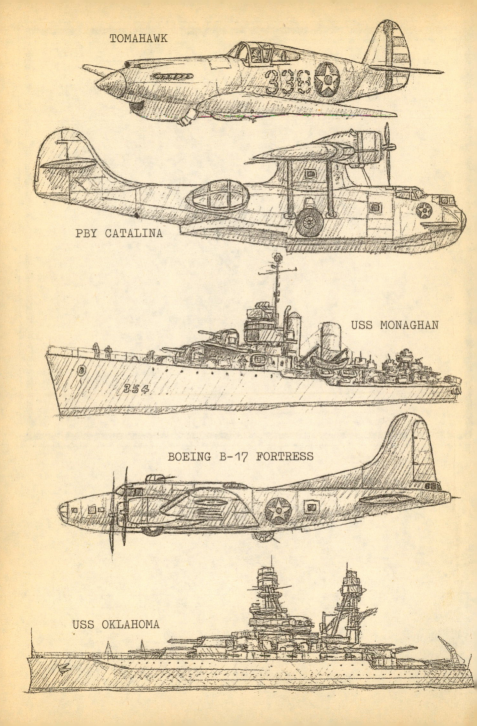

TOMAHAWK

PBY CATALINA

USS MONAGHAN

BOEING B-17 FORTRESS

USS OKLAHOMA

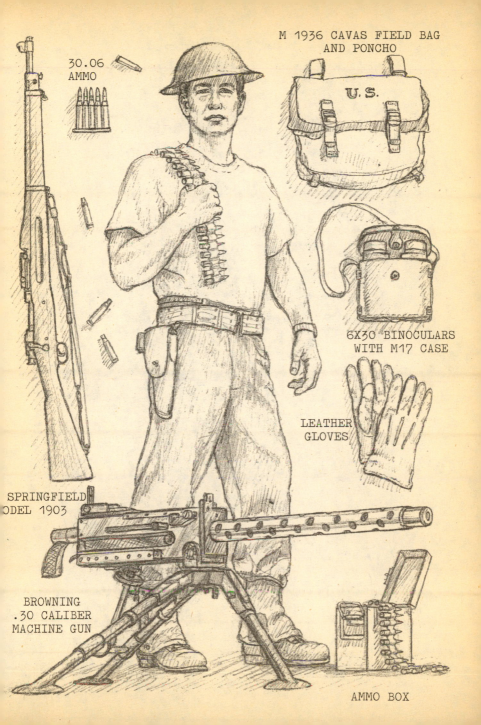

30.06
AMMO

M 1936 CAVAS FIELD BAG
AND PONCHO

U.S.

6X30 BINOCULARS
WITH M17 CASE

LEATHER
GLOVES

SPRINGFIELD
MODEL 1903

BROWNING
.30 CALIBER
MACHINE GUN

AMMO BOX

DOGTAGS

USN M1 KNIFE AND SHEATH

▼ S&W VICTORY MODEL REVOLVER AND HOLSTER

Introduction

On December 7, 1941, Japan attacked Pearl Harbor and other Army and Navy bases in Hawaii. More than three hundred Japanese planes swooped over the island, dropping bombs and torpedoes and shooting machine guns.

The attack was all over in two hours. Pearl Harbor and much of the island of Oahu was ruined. It was the worst attack on the United States in nearly two hundred years.

But the story of Pearl Harbor is about much more than bombs and explosions. Thousands of American soldiers and sailors reacted quickly to the sneak attack. Even though they were all taken by surprise, they dropped whatever they were doing to defend their country. And when their friends were hurt, they risked their lives to help them.

I am here to tell you the story — a story about heroes, about courage, and about fighting back with everything you've got.

— G.I. Joe

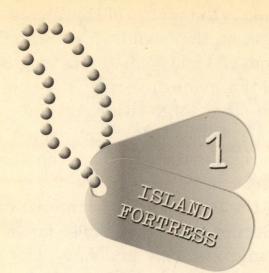

1

ISLAND FORTRESS

Like a chain of green jewels on a blue carpet, the seven islands of Hawaii are lined up in the middle of the Pacific Ocean. The islands have been part of the United States since the 1890s, but in 1941, they weren't an independent state yet. Although Hawaii is separated from the rest of America by about three thousand miles of ocean, in 1941 Hawaiians considered themselves as American as apple pie.

Honolulu is the capital of Hawaii and the largest city on the islands. It is located on the island of Oahu. Along the southern edge of the palm-tree-ringed island of Oahu are other large cities and the main port, Pearl Harbor. Running along the northern ridge of the island are the Koolau Mountains.

Across the Pacific is the island nation of Japan. Beginning in the 1930s, Japan began to build an army and navy. In early 1941, their armies started invading other countries, including Korea and China. To protect Americans, the United States moved more and more American ships, planes, soldiers, sailors, and pilots to Oahu because it was closer to Japan.

In 1941, there were three main parts of the United States' armed forces: the Navy, the Army, and the Army Air Corps. All three parts had stations on Oahu. Navy sailors filled hundreds of ships, Army Air Corps airmen and crews flew and fixed bombers and fighters, and Army soldiers guarded the bases. All were highly trained and most had volunteered for their jobs. Each man and woman in uniform stood ready to do their duty. But no one ever imagined they would have to do that duty so soon or under so much stress.

U.S. Navy

Since 1930, the Navy had kept many ships of all types at Pearl Harbor. The fleet included battleships, the largest fighting ships in the Navy. These enormous ships, each as long as a football field, had huge guns used to fire on land targets and at enemy ships. Each battleship was named for a U.S. state.

Another kind of Navy ship in Pearl Harbor was called a destroyer. These were smaller ships that also had many large guns, but could move more quickly than battleships.

There were dozens of other ships that helped these larger ships work, including oil tankers, tugboats, and supply ships.

There were also submarines, PT boats, cruisers, and more. On December 7, 1941, there were more than 180 different ships filling a jam-packed Pearl Harbor. And all of those ships were loaded with Navy sailors, ready to sail their ships into battle or defend them against attack.

In the center of Pearl Harbor was Ford Island. The Navy had many buildings on this island, including crew housing, a hospital, and supply huts. Also on Ford Island was the Naval Air Station, where the Navy kept its patrol planes, seaplanes, and fighters. Most of the Navy sailors worked on ships, but many others worked on land, helping to supply and organize the many Navy ships.

On the southwest edge of Ford Island was Battleship Row. On December 7, this is where eight of the U.S. Navy's largest and most important battleships were tied up to piers and docks. The huge ships were lined up two by two next to the island. America was not at war in December 1941. These battleships were at Pearl Harbor to help their crews train, and to pick up supplies.

During the attack on Pearl Harbor, Battleship Row was one of the Japanese planes' main targets.

U.S. Army and U.S. Army Air Corps

The U.S. Air Force did not exist in 1941. Instead, pilots and their crews and planes were part of the Army Air Corps. Several places in Hawaii had Army Air Corps airfields and planes.

South of the entrance to Pearl Harbor was Hickam Field. This air base had brand-new barracks, an enormous mess hall for meals, recreational fields, repair shops, hangars, and even a hospital. Hickam also was home to hundreds of Army Air Corps planes called bombers. These planes flew over enemy targets and dropped bombs. The American Army hadn't used their bombers in many years. They hoped they wouldn't have to, but kept them ready just in case. These planes were called B-17s and B-18s; the "B" was for Bomber.

In the center of Oahu was Wheeler Field, another large air base. Wheeler was home to the fast-flying, single-propeller fighter planes called P-40s and P-36s. The "P" stood for "pursuit," which meant that these fast planes would pursue, or chase, enemy aircraft.

More than seven thousand Army Air Corps soldiers, fliers, and other workers were stationed at Hickam, Wheeler, and other Hawaiian airfields.

Near Hickam was Fort Shafter, the home of the Army. These soldiers were not part of the airplane operations of the Air Corps. Their job was to defend all the Army and Army Air Corps bases against attack. They didn't know it when they woke up that morning, but they were going to have a very big job to do on December 7, 1941.

* * *

For all the men and women who worked at these bases or on ships in Pearl Harbor, Hawaii was a dream job. The weather was always beautiful, and the beaches were warm and wide. There were many things for them to do in their off-duty hours. Hickam Field had a movie theater, where servicemen could watch their favorite movies for only a dime. Hundreds of teams played softball, basketball, and other sports. They played ship against ship and base against base. Honolulu had many restaurants that were perfect for sailors and soldiers. At the Black Cat Café in Honolulu, they could enjoy a barbecue beef sandwich and strawberry shortcake for only forty cents.

In the days before December 7, everyone on Hawaii was aware of the threat of Japanese attack. They regularly practiced air raid drills. Even the wives and children of soldiers and sailors who lived on the bases knew where they should go during an attack. Soldiers and sailors also were on alert for spies who might damage planes or buildings.

Many people talked about a Japanese attack, and plans were made to defend the island and the U.S. forces. But no one really seemed to take the threat seriously. The United States of America had not been attacked by a foreign nation since the War of 1812. No one really believed that Japan, a country more than four thousand miles away, could ever attack Pearl Harbor.

On December 7, 1941, a sunny Sunday morning, war seemed a million miles away. Many sailors were at church. Others were getting ready to go golfing or to play baseball on Ford Island. Dozens of officers were at home with their families enjoying a quiet breakfast. A slight breeze off the ocean carried the scent of pineapples. Many American soldiers and sailors thought they were living in paradise.

What they didn't know was that, at that moment, paradise was about to be lost.

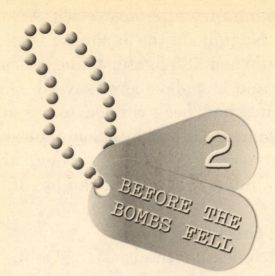

2

BEFORE THE BOMBS FELL

6:10 A.M. to 7:50 A.M.

Just before sunrise on December 7, 1941, people all around Hawaii enjoyed a few more minutes of sleep. Sailors on duty yawned as they looked forward to the end of their watch so they could enjoy the rest of the day. The sun came up rosy and red in the east, and the day looked like it would be just perfect.

At ten minutes after six o'clock, Admiral Chuichi Nagumo of the Japanese Imperial Navy launched 183 fighter planes, torpedo planes, and dive-bombers toward Oahu. The planes had been carried to a spot in the ocean near Hawaii by six Japanese aircraft carriers. It would take them about ninety minutes to reach Hawaii by air.

Aboard the U.S.S. *Ward*

Seven miles off the coast of Oahu, the U.S.S. *Ward*, a Navy destroyer, received a radio report of a submarine sighting. The U.S.S. *Antares*, a supply ship, had spotted the sub near the entrance to Pearl Harbor. Captain William Outerbridge on the *Ward* turned his ship to try to find the sub. The *Ward* soon found the submarine, determined that it was the enemy, and fired on it. A shell hit the tall, thin conning tower of the sub, and it went back under the water. The *Ward* dropped depth charges and tried to sink the sub.

Soon after, Captain Outerbridge's crew

reported that they had indeed sunk the sub. Through his binoculars, he could see large oil patches on the water where it had gone down. The *Ward* continued cruising, many miles off Oahu. The *Antares* waited outside the mouth of Pearl Harbor for orders to enter.

Meanwhile, the *Ward*'s radio room sent a signal to Pearl Harbor that it had attacked and sunk a Japanese sub. This should have been a warning to the U.S. forces, but no one at Pearl Harbor paid much attention to the report. This was the first encounter between American and Japanese forces on December 7. It wouldn't be the last.

Opana Radar Station

High above Pearl Harbor, on the northern coast of Oahu, was a lonely outpost manned on that morning by two Army soldiers. The Opana Radar Station was part of an island-wide network of special radar gear that could see planes and ships from very far away.

Radar was very new in 1941. In fact, Lieutenant Kermit Tyler, who was in charge of Opana Station that December morning, had first seen the machines work only a few weeks earlier.

At about 7 A.M., radar operators told Tyler that a large group of planes was approaching Oahu from the north. Tyler reported this to the Army Information Center.

After several minutes, he reached an officer there who told him that it must be a flight of Army Air Corps B-17s. They were expected to arrive from California that morning. The radar could not tell Tyler and his men what type of planes were coming. So they had to believe the officer's claim.

Lieutenant Tyler and his men did not know it, but they had just spotted the Japanese planes headed for Pearl Harbor to attack the U.S. Navy.

Near Honolulu

On board the U.S.S. *Vestal*, which was docked next to the U.S.S. *Arizona* in Battleship Row, sailors had just finished breakfast and were reading the morning newspaper.

At Hickam Army Information Center, Captain Gordon Blake was in the control tower. He was waiting for the B-17s that had flown overnight from California and were due to arrive any minute.

In downtown Honolulu, early-rising Hawaiians walked past a famous signpost on Kalakaua Avenue. The sign was called the "Crossroads of the Pacific," and showed the distance from Honolulu to many cities around the world. San Francisco and Los Angeles to the east; Sydney, Australia, to the southwest.

And one sign pointing west said, "Tokyo, Japan."

The Japanese attack came without warning. Airplanes poured into the skies above Oahu. Dozens headed for each of the island's important bases. At 7:50 A.M. on that quiet Sunday morning, in the Navy Yard across from Ford Island, Admiral William

Furlong saw a plane flash by his window. A moment later, he heard a loud bang and saw smoke rising from the airfield across the water. He knew at once what was happening.

"We're under attack!" he shouted to his radio operator. "Send this immediately. . . . Man your stations! Air raid! All ships in the harbor, get under way immediately!"

The call went out to all ships: "Air raid Pearl Harbor! This is NOT a drill!"

Loud alarms sounded up and down Battleship Row as lookouts spotted the Japanese planes zooming in from the sea. On every one of the ships at Pearl Harbor, sailors dropped what they were doing and headed for their battle stations.

America was under attack!

3

ATTACKED!

7:51 A.M. to 8:10 A.M.

The Japanese planes swarmed over Oahu like angry bees. And everywhere they passed, they stung — hard.

Kanohe Bay

Kanohe Bay, a tiny Navy airstrip on the central-eastern shore of Oahu, was the very first site struck by Japanese bombs. The strip was the home to several Navy float planes. They were lined up in hangars and around the airfield.

Chief Petty Officer John Finn drove to the Kanohe airfield after hearing some noise from his home nearby. He wasn't sure what to expect when he got to the hangars. What he saw stunned him.

Fires raged and Japanese planes buzzed around the base. They were firing machine guns at planes and men. Chief Finn immediately ran to the gun locker and passed out weapons for the men to fire back. Handguns and rifles wouldn't do much good against fast-flying planes, but they had to do *something*.

He set up a machine gun and manned it himself. For the next twenty minutes he fired at all the planes that zoomed around. Finn was hit by bullets or shrapnel or debris nearly twenty times. Even though he was bleeding from several of the wounds, he continued firing. He knew America needed him.

Wheeler and Hickam Fields

The main targets for the first Japanese bombers were the two largest U.S. airfields. If Japan destroyed American planes, Army Air Corps and Navy fliers wouldn't be able to defend the island against the attacking aircraft.

Japanese planes swooped over Wheeler and Hickam fields again and again. They dropped bomb after bomb onto the planes parked together along the runways. The men on the bases scrambled to get to their battle stations and to put out fires caused by the bombs. Machine guns were unlocked and ammunition was passed to gunners so they could shoot back. Some brave soldiers tried to get the planes out of harm's way.

At Hickam Field, Captain Blake was still in the control tower. Even as the bombs fell all around him, he did his job. He knew that he had to help the flight of B-17s arriving from California land safely. Without his help, they might have crashed. Amid the smoke and noise and fire, he stayed at his post until he had guided all the pilots to a safe landing.

After dropping their bombs, the Japanese pilots flew their planes very low and shot wing machine guns at the planes and buildings. Bullets flew everywhere and men on the ground dove for shelter. Sergeant Steven Koran was running with his wife and baby toward a shelter when he saw a plane heading for them. He pushed his wife and daughter to the ground and dove on top of them. Bullets chewed up the wooden porch they had just been standing on. That was too close for comfort, he thought. He got everyone up and they ran to a concrete shelter. Sergeant Koran made sure the others were safe, then he ran off to his duty station.

All over the airfields, soldiers reacted as

quickly as they could. Within ten minutes of the first enemy planes arriving, U.S. Army and Army Air Corps soldiers were firing back with everything they could get their hands on.

Battleship Row

The main naval targets for the enemy were on Battleship Row next to Ford Island. At 7:55 A.M., the first attackers flew in low over the water and dropped torpedoes. These torpedoes were specially made bombs that hit the water and then zoomed toward their target like underwater missiles.

The *West Virginia* was among the first of the battleships to be stung by torpedoes. Two hit the port, or left, side of the ship, sending up huge towers of water. Almost immediately, the ship began to sink as water poured into the ship. Sailors were told to "abandon ship," and they rushed out of their duty stations. Many leaped directly into the water.

The *Arizona* also received several direct

hits. Flaming debris from these explosions rained down on the *West Virginia* and the nearby *Tennessee*. The *Oklahoma* also was smashed by torpedoes and started listing, or tilting, in the water.

Aboard the U.S.S. *Nevada*

As Japanese planes roared overhead and as fires raged on nearby ships, the Marine band on the *Nevada* began to play "The Star-Spangled Banner" for the daily raising of the American flag. Sailors stood at attention as the flag rose and the band played on. Japanese planes tried in vain to shoot the flag. Bullets ripped into the Stars and Stripes, but the flag reached the top of the pole.

The second the band finished, they dropped their instruments and ran for their stations. But not one man moved during the song. Every Marine stood in place until the flag was raised. That flag flew above the *Nevada* for the rest of the day.

Navy Yard South of Ford Island

Dozens of ships were at piers in the Navy Yard. Many were under repair or loading supplies. Japanese bombers aimed their deadly drops onto the tightly packed ships, and many of the vessels were hit. The battleship *Pennsylvania* was in dry dock and unable to move; it was hit by several bombs.

Sailors on the destroyer U.S.S. *Bagley* watched all this. Then they watched several torpedoes head toward their boat. There was nothing they could do but watch as the torpedoes slammed into the ship's side. Many of the men were thrown to the deck as the ship shuddered from the impact. But they jumped up instantly, shook off their injuries, and manned the machine guns. After one Japanese torpedo plane launched a shot toward the *Oklahoma*, the *Bagley*'s men opened up with a deck machine gun. They fired again and again, tracking the plane as it flew by. Finally, with a huge *POW!* and a giant splash, the bomber smacked into the harbor. Score one for our side, the men said. But they had no time to celebrate. A long and horrible morning was just beginning.

Battleship Row

The torpedo that the *Bagley*'s men had seen heading toward the *Oklahoma* was one of many that hit the huge ship. Within minutes of the first Japanese planes arriving, the *Oklahoma* was hit several times in vital areas below the waterline. The men on board felt the ship tilting more and more. Soon, the deck was tilted at a sharp angle, flinging men into the water. Just after 8 A.M., the *Oklahoma* capsized, turning completely upside down. The *Oklahoma*'s crew scrambled to escape into the oil-clogged water and to swim to safety on Ford Island or another ship.

Among the many brave men on the *Oklahoma* were two young sailors who gave their lives saving others. Ensign Francis Flaherty and Seaman First Class Richard Ward refused to abandon their positions. They held flashlights that helped those trapped belowdecks to escape. Many men were saved, but Flaherty and Ward didn't make it out.

Farther north along Battleship Row, the *Nevada* was trying to fight back, even as fires burned on several places on her deck. Machine gunners fired as quickly as they could. The port-side deck gunners at the bow, or forward part of the boat, shot down a Japanese torpedo plane just one hundred yards from the side of the *Nevada*. The sailors could see right into the cockpits of the planes as they flew low over the water. One sailor said he saw a Japanese pilot wave at him and smile beneath his safety goggles.

Meanwhile, the *Nevada* was trying to move. It took a battleship a long time to build up enough steam to start its huge propellers turning. By chance, the *Nevada* had already been building up steam for an exercise when the attack came. Lieutenant Commander Francis Thomas on the *Nevada* knew that a moving target would be harder to hit. He gave the order to get the ship moving away from the dock.

There was one big problem: the *Nevada* was still tied to the dock by huge ropes. The *Nevada* had to be untied or it couldn't go anywhere.

Elsewhere on Battleship Row, deep inside the *California*, rescue efforts went on to save men trapped by explosions. Lieutenant Jackson Pharris knew that some men were trapped in a room filling up with oily water. Again and again, he swam through the water to get the men out. He was knocked out twice by heavy fumes, but both times he woke up and went right back to help. Scenes of bravery like that one were found all over Pearl Harbor that morning.

Schofield Barracks: Army

Schofield Barracks, the home to hundreds of Army personnel and their families, was quiet until Japanese Zeroes swooped out of the dawn sky. The Zero was the main fighter plane of Japan. Rather than drop bombs, Zeroes used machine guns. The Zeroes flew low, shooting at the buildings on the ground.

As soon as they heard the enemy planes, Lieutenant Stephen Salzman and Sergeant Lowell Klatt raced to their stations at Schofield Barracks. Suddenly, they saw two planes heading right for them. They weren't sure if they were American or Japanese planes. A burst from the planes' guns answered the question for them. Ignoring the danger, they grabbed a pair of Browning automatic rifles (BARs), knelt down in the road, and started firing at the attackers.

One plane was hit by many of their rifle shots. It started smoking, and crashed behind a nearby building. You just make do with what you've got, Klatt thought as he raced forward.

Battleship Row

Fires burned on most of the ships on Battleship Row. The water around the ships was filling with oil that was leaking from holes made by torpedoes. More torpedo planes continued to dive toward the ships. The Japanese planes raced through bullets and shells, but on they came.

The *Oklahoma* had rolled over, the *California* was taking on water fast, and the *West Virginia* was almost completely swamped.

The *Arizona* was leaning over, having been hit by many bombs. Her men fired back at Japanese planes, ignoring the roaring flames around them and the ping of bullets off the metal deck.

Then, at about 8:06 A.M., a lone Japanese plane flew high above the *Arizona* and dropped another bomb. It hit the main deck near the front of the huge ship. The bomb went into the main magazine, or ammunition storage hold, of the *Arizona*.

Seconds later, the *Arizona* blew up. The enormous fireball soared into the sky above Pearl Harbor and could be seen for miles.

This was the saddest moment of the Pearl Harbor attack, and perhaps the saddest moment in U.S. Navy history. That one bomb killed more than one thousand sailors on the *Arizona* and on nearby ships. The *Arizona* sank within minutes. Her tall control tower and bridge were still visible above the water even as her bottom rested on the muddy harbor floor.

Only moments after the attack began, Japan had sunk one of America's great ships.

4

RAYS
OF HOPE

8:11 A.M. to 8:39 A.M.

The attack on the ships in Pearl Harbor continued, but the attacks at the airfields slowed down as Japanese planes headed back out to sea. One of the first things that soldiers at the airfields did was help the wounded.

Hickam Field Hospital/
Tripler Army Hospital

Doctors and nurses at Hickam knew that their jobs would be hard. As soon as the attack was announced over their radios, they hurried to the hospital to prepare for the wounded.

As injured people started pouring in, the staff struggled to keep up. Two surgeons operated nonstop for the rest of the day. A dentist even had to do emergency surgical duty. Rooms quickly filled up with patients. Anyone who could still walk waited outside on the porch.

At Tripler Army Hospital at Wheeler Field, surgeons came from all over Oahu. One doctor was in town from California to give a lecture. He had just begun his class about modern methods of treating wounds when the attack began. "Class dismissed," he said, and headed to the hospital to put his lessons into practice.

There were many heroes at Pearl Harbor. The doctors, nurses, corpsmen, and other hospital workers deserved special thanks. Because they weren't trained to fight, they served their country the best way they knew how: by helping others.

Wheeler Field

On the northern beaches of Oahu there was a tiny airstrip called Haleiwa. The morning of the raid, Army Air Corps Lieutenants George Welch and Kenneth Taylor had left their planes at Haleiwa after a training run and driven back to Wheeler Field.

As soon as the attack began on December 7, both young pilots scrambled into a tiny roadster and sped away toward their planes, eleven miles away. Dodging bomb craters, Zero fighters' bullets, and fires burning along the road, they roared those eleven miles in less than ten minutes.

Welch and Taylor had been out late the night before and had slept in their clothes. So two of the first pilots to take to the air against Japan at Pearl Harbor did so wearing tuxedoes.

North of Ford Island

On the north side of Ford Island was an old destroyer, the U.S.S. *Utah*. For the last few months, she had been used as a target ship by U.S. planes. Her tiny crew just kept her floating to steam around the ocean and get hit with practice bombs.

A Japanese torpedo hit the *Utah* early in the battle. Her officers got the crew on deck right away, but the ship quickly begin to fill with water and turn over. Far below the deck, Chief Water Tender Peter Tomich was at his station. He knew the ship was in serious trouble. He told his men to get out, and get out fast! He knew that if the giant, hot boilers weren't shut off, they would explode when covered by the cold, rising sea water. The explosion would destroy the ship and her crew.

Tomich stayed behind to turn off the boilers. The last time his men saw him, he was busy turning off valves as the ship slowly rolled over. He never made it out.

Aboard the U.S.S. *Nevada*

While fighting off Japanese planes, the *Nevada* fired up her engines. The ship sent a crew of men in a small boat to cut the lines that tied them to the dock. The men chopped the lines with axes. Chief Boatswain's Mate Edwin Hill led the group on to the dock. As the lines fell away, he leaped into the oily water and swam back to the ship. He climbed back up one of the ropes hanging from the ship's side. Hill wasn't going to let the *Nevada* leave without him, even though he would have been safer on Ford Island.

The sight of the mighty battleship steaming proudly down Battleship Row, surrounded by enemy planes, was inspiring for all who saw it. Sailors on the other battleships cheered as the *Nevada* eased through the water. From Hickam Field, soldiers could see the huge gray ship as it glided past, down the channel.

We're still here, the ship seemed to say, we're still in this fight. You can knock us down, but we'll get right back up. The brave sailors on the *Nevada* gave everyone at Pearl Harbor hope that there was fighting spirit left in the Navy.

Flapping proudly from the stern of the *Nevada* was the bullet-scarred American flag, still waving in the face of the enemy.

5

FIGHTING
BACK!

8:40 A.M. to 8:50 A.M.

The Navy wasn't the only service fighting back against the Japanese invaders. The Army Air Corps began to get its turn, too.

Above Wheeler Field

Roaring toward Wheeler Field in their P-40s, Lieutenants Welch and Taylor looked for enemy aircraft. They found lots of targets.

They spotted a group of Japanese Zero fighters shooting at U.S. soldiers on the ground. That's not a fair fight, the American pilots thought. Let's even up the odds.

Zooming to attack speed, the two Army Air Corps pilots fired their guns on the Zeros. Taylor nailed two planes right away, while Welch got a pair as well. In the dogfight, both pilots used up all of their bullets and most of their fuel. They landed to get more.

Crews quickly loaded the two fighters with more ammo and fuel, and Welch took off first. He circled above, waiting for Taylor. But suddenly, Japanese planes attacked the airfield again. Taylor roared into the sky, a Japanese plane hot on his tail. Welch saw the trouble and quickly got behind the Japanese plane. He blasted it out of the sky. Taylor was wounded in the attack, but continued to fly. By the end of the day, Welch shot down four enemy planes and Taylor got three.

America's fighter pilots were fighting back!

Hickam and Wheeler Fields

As Captain Russell Waldron headed to the barracks to check on his men, he heard a loud whistling sound. That meant only one thing: A bomb was falling nearby. He dove to the ground, then heard a huge boom and felt the ground bounce. Shrapnel zinged over his head. If he hadn't made that dive, he would have been hit.

He continued on, diving to the ground each time he heard the whistle. He even had to dive when he actually saw a line of bombs falling toward him. Each time, he dove and made it.

He finally reached the barracks, but all he found was a large group of women and children, confused and scared. As a truck drove by, he jumped in front of it and made the driver stop. He pushed the civilians onto the truck and ordered the driver to "Head for the hills!" and safety. Then he ran back to his duty station where his planes were waiting.

A similar scene happened at Wheeler Field, where Sergeant James Henderson rounded up a group of children who were standing on the street watching the action. He shoved them into a house just before a Japanese plane shot up the street. Then he joined others in shooting back at the enemy plane.

A little after 8:45 A.M., a strange quiet came from the skies above Oahu. No more Japanese planes were heard overhead. Fires raged on ships, in hangars and barracks, and in downtown Honolulu. But the attack had stopped for the moment.

6

ATTACKED...
AGAIN!

8:50 A.M. to 9:45 A.M.

Wheeler Field

The sky was empty for the moment as Japanese planes headed back to their aircraft carriers. American soldiers and pilots worked hard to fix planes. They had to get more planes in the air to defend the island. Many planes were burning wrecks, but some could still fly. Ignoring the danger from the fires and from exploding ammunition, ground crew members worked tirelessly to prepare some P-40s.

There were many more pilots than there were airplanes, so it became a sort of race to see who could get into a plane the fastest. Lieutenants Lewis Sanders, Phillip Rasmussen, and two others formed a flight of four that took off a few minutes before 9 A.M.

While in the air, they were among the first to spot what the whole island feared most: *Another attack! The "second wave" of Japanese planes was bearing down on Oahu!*

Above Wheeler Field

In their P-40s, Rasmussen and Sanders immediately engaged the enemy. The P-40s zoomed through the sky, banking back and forth through the clouds. They were trying to avoid being shot while trying to shoot the enemy Zeroes. One of the U.S. pilots was hit and crashed into the sea. The other three nailed two of the Zeroes and chased others off before returning to base for more ammunition.

That day, more than twenty Japanese planes were shot down by a handful of U.S. planes. Compared to what the United States lost that day, it wasn't much. But the sight of U.S. planes up there doing their best was an inspiration to everyone who saw it.

Aboard the *Nevada*

Under attack by the second wave of planes, the *Nevada* was filling with water and was on fire. But her brave action had saved many other ships from attack. Japanese pilots wanted to sink her in the Pearl Harbor channel. If they had, the harbor might have been blocked for months.

Losing power, and to avoid blocking the harbor, Lieutenant Commander Thomas ordered the *Nevada* to run aground at Hospital Point, southeast of Ford Island. He rammed the ship into the mud and ordered the anchor dropped. The ship was now safely out of the channel. He had accomplished his mission by getting underway and drawing fire away from other ships.

Navy Yard

All over the island, U.S. forces battled back. But Japanese planes dropped more bombs.

About 9:30, fires inside the destroyer U.S.S. *Shaw* burned as it sat at the end of the Navy Yard piers. In a huge explosion, the *Shaw* blew up. A large pillar of flame and smoke rose up over the ship and the Navy Yard, bright red and yellow against the black smoke from other fires.

Sailors nearby were thrown to the ground as the pier and surrounding land seemed to bounce up in the air with the force of the blow. It was loud enough to be heard above the din of fighting as far away as Ford Island and Hickam Field.

Some of the fires at Pearl Harbor, including the one on the *Arizona,* would burn for two or three more days.

North Side of Ford Island

After the *Utah* had rolled over early in the attack, survivors from the ship had gathered on Ford Island. From just yards away on shore, they watched as their ship sunk lower and lower in the mud.

Finally, as the last planes left the area and it was safe to move around, some of the men heard sounds from inside the *Utah.* They realized someone had survived, and was trapped in an air pocket inside the upside-down hull. They found a special metal-cutting torch. Working quickly, they burned a hole in the thick, steel hull near where the sound was coming from.

Inside, Fireman Second Class Jack Vaessen used a wrench to bang on the wall of the room he was trapped in.

Finally, the men outside cut through, and daylight and fresh air poured in to

Vaessen. It was the first rescue from inside a ruined ship that day. It would not be the last. Hundreds of soldiers and sailors pitched in and tried to save the rest of their trapped comrades. They couldn't save all of them, but they saved as many as they could.

By just about 10 A.M., the last Japanese planes had left Oahu airspace, and the attack was over. From start to finish, it had lasted about two hours. To those who were in the middle of the inferno, it had seemed like a lifetime.

Conclusion

The end of the attack . . . the beginning of the recovery.

As the attack slowly ended, small boats rushed out into the oil-choked waters to rescue survivors. Sailors wearing only swim trunks drove motorboats through flaming water to reach people. One ship, the mine-sweeper *Tern*, picked up forty-five men in just a few minutes.

The rescue of men trapped in the ships

and in the water continued far into the night.

Later in the day, dozens of Hawaiian citizens reported to the hospitals to help in any way they could. The lines for donating blood formed as soon as the final planes left. The lines were hundreds of people long for the rest of the week. People of all races, ages, and backgrounds donated their blood to help the wounded.

Around Pearl Harbor, smoking wrecks of American ships floated in ruins at docks and piers at the Navy Yard and around Ford Island. At Wheeler Field, hangars, planes, and barracks burned. At Hickam Field, the wounded were helped and repairs on damaged planes began immediately.

The *California*, the *West Virginia*, the *Oklahoma*, the *Utah*, and the *Arizona* were total losses. The *Nevada* was seriously damaged, but was eventually repaired. Nearly twenty other ships were seriously damaged or sunk.

The Army Air Corps lost more than 188 planes at Wheeler and Hickam fields.

Of course, the greatest losses were people. More than 2,500 people lost their lives, including more than 1,100 on the *Arizona* alone. Another 1,800 people were wounded.

But amid all the damage and destruction was one thought: *We're ready to fight back.* Rather than scare America with their terrible sneak attack, the Japanese had given us strength.

No matter what was thrown at us, we stood up and fought back. It's never easy to fight back, but fighting back is easier when you know you are in the right.

That strength carried America and her Allies to victory in World War II over the forces of Japan, Germany, and Italy. Someone else started the fight . . . but we finished it.

— G.I. Joe

Author's Note

The stories in this book are taken from many sources, including books, Web sites, magazine articles, and movies. As much as possible, they are truly reported here. These are not made-up stories; these were real people placed in real danger. It wasn't easy for them to do their duty while planes were shooting and bombing them, but they did. It cost many of them their lives.

Fourteen people won the Congressional

Medal of Honor at Pearl Harbor, and hundreds more were decorated for their bravery under fire.

Today in Pearl Harbor, you can tour the U.S.S. *Arizona* memorial, which was built directly above the sunken battleship. Parts of the ship are still visible from the deck of the memorial. It stands as a constant reminder of the price freedom pays to fight against evil.

USS ARIZONA MEMORIAL